NO WAY!

It was as awkward as she thought it would be. When they got into the cinema, Jessie left Mum and Steve in the queue and went to get a tub of popcorn and some coke. Then she rejoined them.

Steve suddenly put an arm round Mum's shoulder. And Mum put her arm round his waist.

Jessie stiffened.

When Mum saw her staring at them she dropped her arm guiltily. 'All right, Jess?' she said. And put an arm round her shoulder.

'Do you think you've got enough to keep you going?' Steve said jokingly. Looking at the popcorn.

Jessie glared at him, hugging the tub. She wished he wasn't here with them.

Then Steve and Mum began talking to each other. Quietly. And she couldn't catch what they were saying.

She flicked a piece of popcorn into the air. Mum glanced at her. 'Don't, luvvy,' she said quietly.

Jessie didn't know why, she didn't usually do this sort of thing, but she flick

Sue Vyner

First published in this edition in 2010 by Evans Brothers Limited
2A Portman Mansions
Chiltern Street
London W1U 6NR

British Library Cataloguing in Publication Data
Vyner, Sue.
    No way. — (On the wire)
    1. Mothers and daughters—Juvenile fiction. 2. Broken
homes—Juvenile fiction. 3. Children's stories.
    I. Title II. Series
    823.9'14-dc22

    ISBN-13: 9780237542610

Series Editor: Bryony Jones
Design: Calcium
Photography: Shutterstock

Chapter One

What a great day they'd had today, Jessie thought as she lay in bed. Herself, Jude and Mum. Just the three of them. She closed her eyes and let memories of the day flood through her.

They'd been to the Galleries of Justice. A genuine old court-house and prison. Open to the public to "experience" justice in the past.

And it was brilliant. She smiled to herself in the dark.

On arrival, visitors were asked for a volunteer to "stand trial". And Jude had offered.

Seeing her sixteen-year-old sister standing in the dock in a courtroom, accused of stealing, had been scary. Despite it being a set-up. Another volunteer had read out a prosecution statement. Yet another, a statement in her defence. But Jude was found guilty and sentenced to a public flogging. Followed by deportation to Australia.

It had taken Jessie's breath away. Even now, thinking about it, she tensed.

Each visitor had then been given the identity of a

criminal from past records and was taken down to the cells. Everyone laughing nervously on the way down. And everyone, even the grown-ups, jumping when a dummy figure in old-fashioned costume suddenly moved and turned out to be a live "jailer".

He'd herded them all behind a metal barrier and locked them in. Then told them that the first thing to happen to them would be that their heads would be shaved. 'We sell the hair. For wig-making,' he'd barked in character, before directing his gaze at Jessie. 'Unless you have head lice,' he'd said accusingly. She'd blushed furiously.

He took them down, then, to the actual cells where prisoners had been incarcerated. And took them inside one. Everyone was shocked. It was so tiny. And so dark. Several prisoners, apparently, would have been bundled in together. A hammock for anyone who could afford to pay for its use. 'For obvious reasons,' he'd said. The rest sleeping on the stone floor which was covered with filth. There wasn't a toilet.

Then, with a grin, the jailer had closed the door shut on them with a loud clunk. For "further appreciation of conditions". Jessie had felt a real panic till the door was opened again.

Next, they were taken to an exercise yard, where they saw real names scratched into the brickwork on the walls. Staring at the names, Jessie had wondered about the people who'd scratched them and the misery each name represented. A "matron", also in old-fashioned costume,

then inspected them, before parading them round the yard, yelling at them, marching them round in unison.

Jessie curled up tight and hugged her arms round her. The happy memories of the day suddenly became blurred with an old familiar ache in her belly. The jailer and the matron both reminded her of her father.

All three of them in the same mould. Bullies. She tried to push the thought away. Not wanting to spoil the happy mood she'd been in. She rocked herself gently.

It always came back to Dad, she thought. Even though it was over a year now since he'd left, there still weren't many days when thoughts of him didn't push their way into her mind.

Bullying, she decided, should be a crime. Her dad deserved to be punished for the way he'd treated her and Jude and Mum.

She imagined him standing in the dock.

'He's a bully,' she'd say for the prosecution. 'Always shouting at us. And threatening us. Raising his fist. And worse, my lord.'

'Worse? Tell us about it,' the prosecution would say.

'He hit my mum and knocked her over.'

'He was drunk,' his defence would say.

But. 'That's no defence,' the judge would say. And pronounce him, 'Guilty as charged.'

So what about punishment then? she now wondered. A public flogging? It was what he deserved. But the thought made Jessie bury her head under the covers. She hated

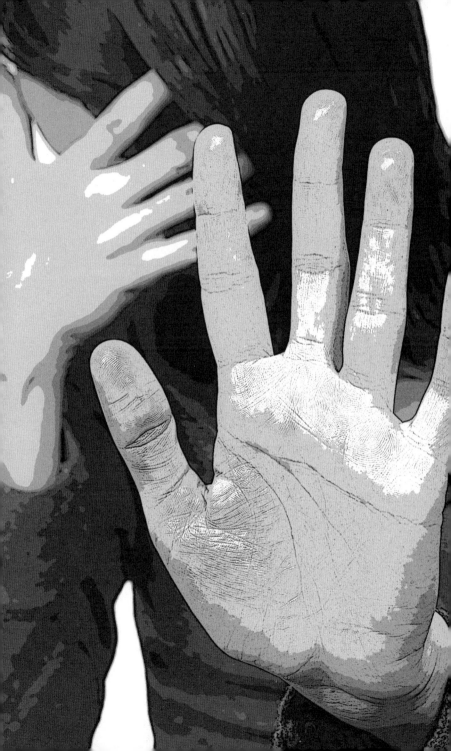

violence. It scared her. Just thinking about it now, her stomach knotted in fear.

Fear was one of the feelings she most associated with her father. Fear of his long uncomfortable silences, which were usually the build-up to a row. Fear of his ranting when the row broke – of what he might do next. Especially when he'd had a drink. Which usually led to more drink. Leading to drunken rages.

Jessie stuck her head out of the covers and gulped at the air.

The day he hit Mum had been the worst. She could still see Mum sprawled on the floor. And she would never forget the look on her face. "*That's it!*" she'd said in an icy voice. And while Dad slept off the drunken rage, she'd packed his bags. When he woke she told him to leave or she'd go to the police.

He'd left and returned a few days later. That becoming a pattern for a while. But each time Mum held out and said she didn't want him back, until in the end, he'd gone for good.

The relief! It helped Jessie relax and a long slow breath helped undo the knot in her stomach.

So. No public flogging for her dad, she thought. But the idea of him being sent away to the other side of the world appealed to her.

Anyway, he'd gone now. Problem over. And all three of them delighted. Mum and her and Jude. 'Girls together,' Mum'd often say now. Smiling.

Jessie told herself to *stop* thinking about him now. To concentrate instead on thinking about how they'd spent the rest of the day. How they'd sat at a pavement café in town, drinking and eating and watching the world go by. Like they didn't have a care in the world. Brilliant.

Jessie felt herself drifting off to sleep at last. Happy with the way things had turned out. Hoping they would never change.

Chapter Two

But then, things did begin to change.

Mum started acting strangely. Suddenly wearing make-up to work. Fussing every morning with her hair. And agonising over what to wear.

Then she started talking about "this guy".

Straight away Jessie was on tenterhooks. She didn't want any "guy" interfering in their life now.

At first he didn't have a name. Mum'd just say that she'd had coffee at work with "this guy". Then when she was late home she'd say that she'd had a quick drink after work with "this guy".

Before long, "this guy" began to feature more and more in her conversations.

Auntie Brenda, Mum's sister, said she was glad that Mum was getting out. But Jessie became more and more edgy. Fear pushing its way into her life again. Fear of something bad starting over again.

Then Jude got herself a boyfriend. Tyrone. Her first proper boyfriend. And soon Jude was acting up too.

Suddenly having no time for anyone or anything else. Especially her sister.

Jessie felt left out of everything. And she hated it.

One afternoon when Mum got home from work, she called the girls downstairs. 'I'm going out tonight. With Steve. You girls will be all right on your own, won't you?' she said.

So he had a name now, Jessie thought. And they were going out on a proper date. She swallowed hard.

'I am sixteen, Mum,' Jude said indignantly. 'We hardly need a babysitter.'

But she looked put out.

Jessie knew that look on her sister's face. It meant a major sulk. Jude obviously wasn't happy staying in with her tonight. Something to do with Tyrone, no doubt. Well, Jessie thought, there was no need for anyone to stay in on her account.

'I don't need a babysitter either,' she said firmly. 'I'm thirteen. I can stay in on my own.'

But Mum shook her head. 'No, you can't,' she said equally firmly.

Which made Jessie mad too. 'I don't want anyone putting themselves out for me,' she snapped. Feeling herself going red in the face. 'I don't want to spoil *anyone's* fun.'

Now Mum turned on Jude. 'You're being selfish, Jude,' she said. 'Just because I want you to stay in for one night.'

'But I didn't say anything,' Jude insisted. Her chin jutting out.

Before Jessie knew it, there was a row in progress.

'But you may as well have,' Mum retorted. 'The look on your face was enough.'

They were all shouting now.

'You're only young once, Mum,' Jude yelled.

'So you can go out every night. I can't go out once,' Mum said. Her voice high-pitched. 'And I'm not so old either,' she added.

Jessie rushed out of the room. She dashed up to her bedroom and threw herself on the bed.

Things had been so all right since Dad left. Why did they have to change now? She clenched her fists.

When a car door slammed she jumped off the bed and went to look out of the window.

She couldn't see him properly. So she rushed to the landing. Just as the door bell rang.

Mum opened the door.

He stepped inside.

After saying something she couldn't hear, Mum called, 'Steve wants to say hello.' Her voice edgy.

Jude appeared just as Jessie reached the bottom of the stairs.

He looked quite trendy. His clothes. The peak of hair sticking up at the front.

'This is Steve,' Mum said.

'Hi, girls,' he said.

Jude mumbled something.

Jessie eyeballed him.

Mum pecked the girls on the cheek. Slung her coat over her shoulder. 'See you later,' she said. Walking to the door self-consciously.

As he went through the door, Steve turned round. Grinned. And winked at the girls. Like it was a game.

Jessie took an instant dislike to him. 'Huh!' she said to Jude when the door closed. 'What do you think to him then?'

But Jude was still in sulk mode. And she never had much to say in sulk mode. She shrugged.

'We'll just have to get used to it,' she said.

'No way!' Jessie said firmly.

But Jude was already on her way upstairs.

Jessie went up to her own room and sank on to the bed. Since Dad had left, it'd felt like she could breathe easy. And the thought of all that friction starting over again was making her feel sick. She sniffled. Dragged the back of her hand across her wet nose.

She had a dad she never wanted to see again. A sister who cared more about a boyfriend than she did about her. And a mother who was behaving like a teenager.

What was going to happen next?

She buried her head in her pillow.

Chapter Three

A few days later Mum was going out with him again.

Jessie sat in her bedroom listening to Mum getting ready. She slammed a cupboard door. Mum hated slamming doors. Then she slammed another door to make the point that she was angry. She waited for Mum to yell at her.

There was a tap on the door and Mum came in. 'What are you doing tonight, Jess?' she said. Sitting down on the bed.

She looked nice.

'Nothing,' Jessie said.

'Homework?' Mum said.

'I've always got homework,' Jessie said sulkily.

Mum looked thoughtful. 'What about a day out at the weekend. All of us?' she said.

'Yesss!' Jessie said. Breaking into a grin. Remembering the great day they'd had at the Galleries of Justice.

'Steve wants to take us somewhere. A chance for him to get to know you,' Mum said.

Jessie's face dropped. Her bottom lip quivering like when she was a little girl. 'I didn't know you meant him as well,' she said.

Mum got hold of her and hugged her.

'Why can't it be just the three of us?' Jessie said. Snuggling up to Mum. Soft. Smelling nice. 'Like when we went to the Galleries of Justice. That was a great day, wasn't it?'

Mum nodded. 'And this will be a great day too,' she said. There was a pause. 'Steve's got a little girl. Tracey. She's nearly five. He wants us to meet her, too.'

This was even worse than Jessie thought. Mum must have felt the shudder go through her because her arms tightened round her.

But Jessie pulled away from Mum and stared up at her. Eyes glaring.

'I don't want to go out with him or his kid,' she said.

Mum dropped her eyes.

Jessie suddenly thought about Mel, her best friend. Mel and her mum had always been on their own. She gulped. 'Mel and her mum've been on their own forever,' she said. 'They're happy as they are.'

Mum looked at Jessie. Her eyes appealing. 'When you get to know Steve I think you'll like him,' she said.

Which panicked Jessie. It all sounded so – inevitable. 'But I like it as we are,' she said. 'You don't understand Mum, I don't want to get to know him.'

Mum pulled Jessie to her again and kissed the top of

her head. 'I understand more than you think, Jess. We had a bad time with your dad. And it's hard to forget that. Nobody knows that better than me.' She sighed. 'But not all relationships are like that, you know.'

So it was a *relationship* now, Jessie thought. Things were sounding more serious by the minute. 'It's the only relationship I know,' she said. Her voice cracking.

Mum held her tight. 'And I feel bad about that. I do so want things to be better now, Jess,' she whispered.

Jessie pulled away, looked directly into Mum's eyes. 'You've no need to feel bad about it, Mum. It wasn't your fault,' she said fiercely. 'And things have been better. They've been brilliant,' she said. 'That's why I don't want them to change.'

Mum sighed. Stood up. 'You'll have to trust me on this, Jess,' she said gently. Making for the door. 'There's a box of Maltesers in the cupboard for you,' she said. Changing the subject. 'Might help the homework along.'

But Jessie couldn't concentrate on her homework. Thoughts flashing through her head like scenes at a cinema. What about this kid, then? Four! Kids at that age were a real pest.

And what about this kid's mother? Had Steve treated them badly? Is that why they weren't together anymore?

She just didn't get it. Dad had given Mum *such* a hard time. How could Mum risk it happening again?

She wandered downstairs. Switched on the telly. Anything to distract her.

There was a knock on the back door. It was Tyrone.

She shouted to Jude. Jude shouted for him to go upstairs.

Now Jessie felt more miserable than ever. Tyrone and Jude together. Mum and Steve together. And her on her own. She felt left out and excluded. And it was a feeling she'd been having a lot lately. She suddenly felt very lonely.

The evening dragged on.

When Tyrone left, Jude came downstairs. 'You should be in bed,' she said to Jessie.

Huh! The only reason her sister bothered to acknowledge her at all was to boss her around. Jessie ignored her.

'Did you hear me?' Jude repeated.

'I'm not tired,' Jessie said. Sitting tight. 'And what do you think about Saturday then?' she added.

Jude looked blank.

So Mum had told her first, then. Jessie was glad. It was one over on her sister. 'She wants us to go out. With him,' she said.

'What a bore,' Jude said.

'And his *kid's* coming too,' Jessie added. 'Did you know he had a kid?' she asked. 'Four years old. Huh!'

But Jude was watching telly now.

'Don't you care?' Jessie shouted.

Jude was still watching the telly.

'Hello! Is anyone there?' Jessie yelled.

'It's your bedtime,' Jude reminded her. 'You'll be in trouble if you're not in bed by the time Mum gets home.'

'You can't tell me what to do. When to go to bed,' Jessie snapped.

'Fine. If you want to get into trouble it's up to you,' Jude said.

And when Mum came home she *was* cross. 'It's school tomorrow, Jessica. And you won't want to get up in the morning. You'll be evil,' she said.

Mum only called her Jessica when she was angry. Jessie pushed out her bottom lip.

'Told you,' Jude said.

Jessie got out of the chair. Stood. Arms folded, shoulders slumped. 'Everyone's angry these days,' she said.

'That's not fair, Jess,' Mum said.

'Well. There was a row with Jude before you went out last time,' Jessie accused her. 'And this time, the minute you get in the door you start on me.'

'You're getting off the point. You should be in bed,' Mum said. But her face softened. 'All right. Five minutes.'

Jessie sat down again.

'Did Jessie tell you about Steve taking us out on Saturday, Jude?' Mum said.

Jude pulled a face. 'Yes,' she said. 'I can think of better things to do on a Saturday, Mum,' she wheedled.

Mum looked flummoxed. 'It'll be great,' she said. 'A chance to all get out together. Enjoy ourselves.'

Jessie held her breath. Perhaps if Jude said she didn't want to go either, Mum would call it off. But she didn't. She just sighed.

Mum took it for agreement. 'Steve'll sort it all out, then,' she said.

'But I don't want to go,' Jessie said. Her chin up.

'Please, Jess, don't be so stubborn,' Mum said.

Jessie leapt up and rushed out of the room, slamming the door behind her.

All she could think of as she lay in bed was, how could she get out of going with them on Saturday?

Chapter Four

'You've got to ask me over for the day on Saturday, Mel,' she blurted out to Mel as soon as she saw her at school the next morning. 'Mum wants us to go out with this Steve, doesn't she? *And* his kid.' She rolled her eyes. 'No way!'

'Poor you,' Mel said. Then frowned. 'But I'd have to have a good reason for asking you.'

'I've thought of that,' Jessie said. Grinning. 'We can say that your mum is having this party. And as you'll be the only kid there, you'll be out of it, won't you? Poor thing! And that's where I come in. With me there to keep you company you'll be fine, won't you?' She grinned again. 'Oh. And it'll be best if I come for a sleepover Friday night. Then there'll be no complications about lifts and things on Saturday.'

Mel laughed. 'You've got it all worked out,' she said. 'OK.'

Jessie hugged her.

But when they were having their meal that night, Mum started going on and on about Saturday. 'Steve's got it planned, girls. He's driving us up to the Dales. We'll find a pub. Have a nice meal when we get there. Then walk along the river.'

She was flushed with excitement.

It made it harder for Jessie. She took a quick breath.

'Mel's mum's having this party on Saturday, Mum,' she said. 'For her workmates. Lunch and all that. Mel's been helping with the cooking already. They've been making quiches and sausage rolls and cheesecakes all week.' She was using her arms to gesture, her eyes to exaggerate. 'And so they need me there, don't they? To keep Mel company. Otherwise she'll be completely out of it. The only kid there.' She rolled her eyes. 'It was her mum's idea. *As long as Jessie's there you'll be all right*, she said to Mel.' Jessie took another quick breath.

'So Mel's asked me to go for a sleepover on Friday. And I can be there all day Saturday. So that's me sorted Saturday. I can go, can't I, Mum? Please?'

Mum looked at Jessie. Folded her arms. 'I'm sorry, Jess.' She shook her head very slowly. Very deliberately.

'But...' Jessie started to say.

Mum interrupted her. 'It's our day, Jess. It's all arranged. And I want you to come with us. End of story. I'll ring Mel's mum and explain why you can't go.'

'*It's all arranged. End of story*,' Jessie cried. 'No taking account of my feelings, then.' She was furious. But she knew when she was beaten. 'Forget it. I'll explain to Mel at school.'

Saturday came. Steve arrived to pick them up.

Mum opened the front passenger door and got in the car. Then she turned to look at the small child sitting in the middle of the back seat, eyes down, clutching a bag.

Steve was loading waterproofs and things into the boot. He came round to the driver's door and leaned in. 'This is Lindsey, Jessie and Jude's mum,' he said to Tracey. No response.

'This is Tracey,' he said to Mum.

Mum smiled at Tracey. But Tracey didn't look up. Just kept her head down. Clutching her bag.

Mum smiled at Steve and shook her head gently.

Jude and Jessie got in the back. One each side of Tracey.

It was a squash.

'There's not enough room,' Tracey said. Her voice verging on tears. 'And I don't want to be in the middle.' Her head was still down.

'This is Jude and Jessie,' Steve said cheerfully. 'They've been dying to meet you.'

Jessie's eyebrows shot up. What a cheek!

Steve glanced away guiltily.

Mum smiled nervously. 'We've all been looking forward to meeting you, Tracey,' she said.

More lies! Jessie couldn't believe what she was hearing.

'*I* don't want to meet *any*body,' Tracey said into her lap.

Ditto, Jessie thought.

Tracey shuffled her bottom around to make sure that she took up as much of the seat as possible. 'There's not enough room for three in the back, Daddy,' she said.

Little brat, Jessie thought. How much room did she need?

'All belted up?' Steve asked. Getting in and starting the engine.

Jessie's seat-belt anchor was somewhere under Tracey's bottom. She poked around for it.

'Ow!' Tracey said. 'She pinched my bottom, Daddy.' She looked up now. Dark brown eyes staring out of a small pale face. And if looks could kill!

Jessie scowled back at her. 'No I didn't,' she said. 'I'm trying to do up my seat-belt, that's all. Shove up a bit.'

'Jess,' Mum said warningly.

But Jessie was only trying to find the seat-belt fastening. It wasn't her fault the kid was sitting on it. She continued poking around, Tracey refusing to co-operate by lifting her bottom.

'Ow!' she yelled again and again. Then wailed, 'I told you there wasn't room Daddy, didn't I?'

Steve turned off the engine. Got out of the car. Opened the back door. Leaned over Jessie. She recoiled. The old fear triggered. But all he did was locate the belt anchor and fasten the belt for her. Then he winked at Jessie. She stared back at him. He got back into the driver's seat and started the car again.

As they drove off, Jude got out her iPod, put her ear phones in, and settled back.

That was when Jessie remembered her mobile. Which went everywhere with her. But she had been up late this morning – after all it was the weekend – and everything had been a rush to get ready. And so, she'd actually forgotten her mobile. She couldn't believe it. And she couldn't bear it. 'I want my mobile, I've forgotten my mobile,' she said frantically. Already needing to text Mel.

'Do you want me to go back?' Steve said. But he was now on the main road and already in thick traffic.

'You can do without your mobile for one day, Jess,' Mum said, as if Jessie was making a fuss about nothing.

'Mum!' Jessie said.

Mum turned round and gave Jessie an I-definitely-mean-it look.

Jessie pouted.

Tracey opened her bag. 'I've got my NDS,' she said triumphantly.

Then she looked at Jessie and put her tongue out. Dark eyes glinting.

Jessie narrowed her eyes and whipped out the tip of her tongue too.

'She put her tongue out at me,' Tracey wailed.

'Jessica!' Mum said.

But Jessie felt evil. If she couldn't be with Mel today, at least she wanted to text her.

Chapter Five

They'd only been on the motorway for a few miles when the traffic slowed down to a crawl. Then came to a halt.

Jude's head was moving to her music. Tracey's fingers were flicking over the Nintendo DS. Jessie had nothing to do.

'An accident. Must be,' Steve said. Tapping the steering wheel.

Jessie remembered how it was when Dad was in a traffic jam. First there'd be the bad language. Then he'd wind the window down and shake his fists, shouting and swearing at anyone and everyone. Finally he'd hold his hand on the hooter while trying to manoeuvre round the car in front, all but nudging it. Mum would try her best to soothe him. And then he'd start on her. And Jessie's stomach would tighten with fear.

She waited for Steve to go into the same routine. Except that he just whistled lightly under his breath, tapping the steering wheel and easing gently forward when there was room.

Jessie sighed with relief.

She studied Steve in the rear view mirror. The sticking up hair. The bump on his nose. The crooked mouth.

He suddenly glanced in the mirror and caught her looking at him. He winked at her and Jessie blushed. Mad that he'd caught her looking at him.

She turned and stared out of the side window.

'Shall we play the alphabet game?' Mum said.

Mum loved playing silly games in the car.

Not today Mum, please! Jessie thought. Not in front of these – strangers. 'No, Mum!' she said firmly.

'What about you, Tracey?' Mum said.

'Don't want to,' Tracey said.

Cars as far as the eye could see. In front of them and behind them and at the side of them. Three lanes choc-a-bloc.

'I spy?' Mum suggested brightly.

'Yuk,' Tracey said.

Brat, Jessie thought. It was one thing for *her* to think Mum was daft. Quite another for a four-year-old.

As the hold-up continued, tension inside Jessie increased. She tried to catch Jude's eye. But Jude might as well not have been there for all the company she was. The kid was now fidgeting non-stop. And this guy who she didn't know, and didn't want to, was giving Mum sidelong glances. And Mum was smiling back at him. Yuk!

She stared out of the window. Aching for her mobile. Thinking of what she could be telling Mel. It wasn't fair.

But then at last the traffic thinned out and they got going again. And now Steve put his foot down. Jessie let out a sigh of relief. She couldn't have stood much more of that.

By the time they got off the motorway it was nearly lunch time. And Jessie was starving. She was always bad tempered when she was hungry. She elbowed Tracey in the side. 'Sorry,' she said.

'Daddy!' Tracey yelled.

'Keep an eye out for a pub,' Mum said.

But it was always the same. When you weren't looking for one, you passed them all the time. When you wanted one there wasn't one in sight.

'I'm starved,' Tracey moaned.

For once Jessie agreed with her.

The road stretched on.

Then, 'Just what the doctor ordered,' Steve said with a smile as they saw a pub and pulled into the car park.

How could he be so cheerful? Jessie wondered. And why did it irritate her so much? Perhaps it was because she was so miserable. This man. This kid. She just couldn't connect to either of them. They were nothing to do with her. Strangers. And it felt like they'd never be anything else.

The car park was full. And inside things were no better. They pushed their way through the bar.

'Is there a restaurant area?' Steve asked.

'It's full, but you're welcome to find a table in the bar,' the barman said.

But the bar was crowded and noisy and smoky. Mum shook her head. 'Let's try somewhere else,' she said. Steve ushered them out again.

Tracey pulled on Steve's arm. 'I'm hungry. Why are we going somewhere else?' she said. Stamping her foot.

'Baby,' Jessie said under her breath.

But Tracey heard. 'I'm not a baby,' she yelled. 'She says I'm a baby, Daddy.'

'Of course you're not a baby,' Mum said. And tried to put an arm round Tracey, but she pushed it off.

Jessie glared at her.

'There'll be another pub soon,' Mum said, trying to calm

things down as they piled back into the car and drove on.

No chance, Jessie thought.

However, they eventually saw one. Parked. Piled inside. Again. Through the gloomy interior to the restaurant area. Again. This time spotting an empty table.

They hurried to claim it. Steve and Mum beaming at each other.

Tracey refused to sit down. Instead she clung to Steve. Hanging onto his leg. 'What do you want to eat, Trace?' he asked her.

'You know, Daddy! You've not forgotten, have you?' she said. Her eyes huge.

A stab of sympathy took Jessie by surprise. Tracey probably only saw her dad at weekends. And the kid was worried that he'd forgotten what she liked to eat.

'Sausages and chips. Of course!' Steve said. Tracey's face broke into a smile. The first of the day.

'Of course,' she said.

They ordered. Steve persuaded Tracey to sit down. Then they waited.

And waited.

Jessie sat with her arms folded and kicked her foot against the table leg. If she didn't eat soon she'd die.

Every so often Tracey moaned and asked if her sausages and chips were coming.

Even Jude looked fed up.

Mum kept glancing from one to another of them, giving them all an anxious half-smile. It was painfully obvious how much she wanted everybody to be happy and enjoy themselves, Jessie thought. And felt guilty. They all looked so glum. She made an effort at a smile at Mum.

When the meal did finally arrive, apart from being so hungry, it was pure relief to be doing something. Jessie ate her food as if she'd not eaten for days. As they piled back into the car, clouds began to gather.

'It's going to rain,' Jude said.

'I hate rain,' Tracey complained.

'Nobody likes rain,' Jessie said. Like *anyone* likes the rain, she thought. Stupid kid.

'Some people do,' Tracey said defiantly.

'No, they don't,' Jessie said.

'Dogs do,' Tracey said. Out of nowhere.

Jessie laughed.

'She's laughing at me, Daddy,' Tracey said. And dissolved into tears.

'Jess!' Mum said. Exasperated.

Another half hour's drive and the rolling hills and country roads of the Dales appeared.

'Wow!' Mum said. Turning round and beaming at the three girls.

'It is beautiful,' Steve said, reaching over and putting his hand on Mum's.

Jessie felt a pang of jealousy.

But just as they found a car park, the sun disappeared and threatening clouds scudded over the sky, driven by a cold wind.

Nevertheless, they parked. Got the waterproofs out of the boot. And set off along the riverbank.

As Tracey clung to Steve's hand, he pointed out interesting features to her. And when she began to complain that she was tired, he lifted her up on to his back. Mum walking alongside them. She was talking to Tracey too. Like she used to do to her and Jude, Jessie thought. Another stab of jealousy. Tracey was obviously the centre of their attention.

Jessie and Jude brought up the rear. But when Jessie tried talking to Jude, Jude seemed distracted. Thinking about Tyrone, she supposed. So she deliberately hung back on her own. Actually stopped. Wondering how long it would be before anyone noticed.

They were nearly out of sight, in fact, before Mum glanced round and saw her. Then waited.

So much for a day out for everyone, Jessie thought as she walked slowly towards them. Fuming. No one was bothered whether she was there or not. It had taken them long enough to notice when she wasn't.

'You can't have a piggy back,' Tracey said when she finally caught them up.

Brat, Jessie thought.

What was it about walking that grown-ups liked so much? she wondered as they pushed on further. It was so boring.

Especially when it rained.

At first it was just a drizzle. Soon becoming a downpour.

Then a deluge.

They bolted back to the car. But it seemed much farther going back than coming. Half-carrying, half-dragging Tracey.

Despite their waterproofs, by the time they got back to the car they were all of them soaked inside and out.

They dragged off their waterproofs. Got in the car. Water dripping everywhere. Steve tried to make a joke about it but nobody laughed.

The journey home was even more subdued than the journey there.

Chapter Six

'What a day!' Jessie said to Mel on Monday morning.

Mel chuckled. 'Well, it wasn't like you were expecting to enjoy yourself, were you?' she said. 'So what's he like, then? Tell.'

'He tries,' Jessie admitted.

'So he's OK, then?' Mel said.

'I didn't say that,' Jessie said. Frowning.

'What do you mean then?' Mel said.

But Jessie still wasn't sure about Steve. 'Well. He doesn't get in a rage when things go wrong,' she said. 'That's a bonus. Like in the traffic jam. My dad would've gone mental. But Steve just tapped the steering wheel and waited.'

'It sounds like he's not so bad,' Mel said.

'And he was good with his kid,' Jessie said. 'I don't know how he kept his temper with her.'

'She's that bad, then?' Mel said with a giggle. Jessie's eyes widened.

'Worse. She's a brat,' she said. 'Real trouble.'

'Yet he was good with her?'

Jessie nodded. 'Yes.'

'So. It's not all bad, then?' Mel said.

Jessie shrugged.

Mel suddenly looked thoughtful. A hint of longing in her eyes. 'I've no idea what it's like having a man around,' she said. 'Sometimes...'

She went quiet.

'What?' Jessie said.

'I don't know...' Mel said. 'Sometimes I think it would be OK...'

'If you'd had a dad like mine, you'd never think that,' Jessie said vehemently.

They were both lost in thought for a moment.

'Hasn't your mum ever had a boyfriend, Mel?' Jessie said.

Mel shook her head. 'Every so often the girls at work try to get her off with someone,' she said. 'But it never comes to anything. She seems happy enough going out with the girls.'

'That's great,' Jessie said. Thinking how less complicated things would be if Mum did the same thing.

'Cheer up,' Mel said. 'If this day out was really as bad as you say it was, it will have put him off anyway. So stop worrying.'

But she was wrong...

Later that week, Mum asked Jessie if she'd like to go to the cinema to see the new blockbuster that everyone was talking about. Knowing how much Jessie wanted to see it. Getting her excited. Before letting it slip that *he* was going with them.

Jude was going to see the film with Tyrone anyway. So that left Mum and her and *him*. The three of them. How bad was that?

It was as awkward as she thought it would be. When they got into the cinema, Jessie left Mum and Steve in the queue and went to get a tub of popcorn and some coke. Then she rejoined them.

Steve suddenly put an arm round Mum's shoulder. And Mum put her arm round his waist.

Jessie stiffened.

When Mum saw her staring at them she dropped her arm guiltily. 'All right, Jess?' she said. And put an arm round her shoulder.

'Do you think you've got enough to keep you going?' Steve said jokingly. Looking at the popcorn.

Jessie glared at him, hugging the tub. She wished he wasn't here with them.

Then Steve and Mum began talking to each other. Quietly. And she couldn't catch what they were saying.

She flicked a piece of popcorn into the air. Mum glanced at her. 'Don't, luvvy,' she said quietly.

Jessie didn't know why, she didn't usually do this sort of thing, but she flicked another piece.

This time Mum frowned at her.

Fortunately, the queue started to move.

The cinema filled up quickly. There was a real buzz of excited expectancy. Jessie looked round and saw some faces from school. If *he* wasn't there she'd be so happy. There were catcalls as everyone waited for the lights to go down. And a cheer when they did. The pounding sound-track accompanying the advertisements raised everyone's mood another notch.

She had really been looking forward to seeing this film. But as soon as it started, Mum and *him* got closer. Leaning against each other.

Jessie began to drink her coke making a loud sucking noise through the straw.

That did the trick. Mum leaned away from Steve and towards her, then frowned disapprovingly. Like when Jessie was little. Making Jessie make all the more noise. Like she was little. When Mum frowned at her again, it made her giggle nervously.

Mum definitely wasn't amused. A kid a few seats away was, though. She giggled too, then did the same thing with her drink.

Mum leaned over Jessie. 'You're showing yourself up,' she whispered.

She was showing herself up? When Mum had been sitting there nearly on his knee! That made Jessie really mad. Well. If Mum thought she was showing herself up, she may as well live up to it. She flicked some popcorn over the heads of the row in front.

A kid looked round and flicked some back.

'Stop it,' Mum hissed. 'Stop it, Jessie.'

Steve got hold of Mum's hand and squeezed it as if to say take no notice of her.

Jessie longed to tell him to get off her mum. By now she'd lost the gist of the film. And it felt like she had the devil in her. She slid down the seat, folded her arms, and put her feet up on the seat in front of her. Like she'd seen others do.

Mum leaned over and pushed them down.

Jessie thought she saw a glint in Steve's eye. Was he

going to do a *dad* on her at last? Then Mum would see him for what he was? She put her feet up again.

A man turned round. 'Put your feet down!' he demanded in the middle of a dramatic moment in the film.

A woman along the row shushed.

People were turning round. Looking.

Jessie wished she could sink down into the seat and disappear. She wanted to curl up and die. She hated being the centre of attention.

The film was ruined. And all because of *him*.

She shrank back into the seat. Unable to concentrate on the rest of the film.

Chapter Seven

No one spoke on the way home.

When they got in the house, Mum slumped down onto the settee. 'I don't know what Steve thinks to your behaviour. What got into you, Jessie?' she said.

Jessie, herself, couldn't quite believe she'd behaved so badly. But she wasn't going to admit it. 'It was *his* fault!' she said.

'Pardon me?' Mum said. Her eyes wide. 'I don't think so!'

Jessie stared glumly at the floor.

'You were the one out of line,' Mum said. Her voice accusing.

Then Jessie began to cry. 'I hate him,' she sobbed. And rushed upstairs.

It was a storm of crying. Pouring out of her. Her shoulders twitching, her breathing irregular. When she stopped, she felt wrung out. Laying sprawled on her back on the bed.

She heard Jude come in and Mum and her talking.

She dragged herself off the bed and crept onto the

landing to listen.

'She's mixed up, that's all. She'll come round,' Jude was saying.

'I thought that myself at first. I'm not so sure now.' There was a pause. 'What do you think to Steve, Jude?' Mum said.

'He's OK,' Jude said.

Creep, Jessie thought.

'He's never upset her. Done everything in fact to do the opposite. But Jessie seems to hate him,' Mum said.

'She'll get over it. She's too young to understand,' Jude said. As if *she* wasn't a teenager too.

'But she's not giving Steve a chance,' Mum said.

Jessie nearly fell downstairs in the rush to have her say. 'I'm not too young to understand,' she said through clenched teeth. 'I understand very well. I understand that what *I* think doesn't matter in this family at all.' She paced around angrily.

Mum patted the empty space on the sofa next to her. 'Come and sit down,' she said. Jessie went and sat next to Mum. 'What *do* you think, Jess? I really want to know.'

Here was her chance. But suddenly Jessie felt tongue-tied. 'It was bad before – you know – with Dad –' she began.

Mum nodded.

Jessie searched for the right words. 'No. It was worse than bad. It was –'

'Terrible,' Jude said. Nodding encouragingly.

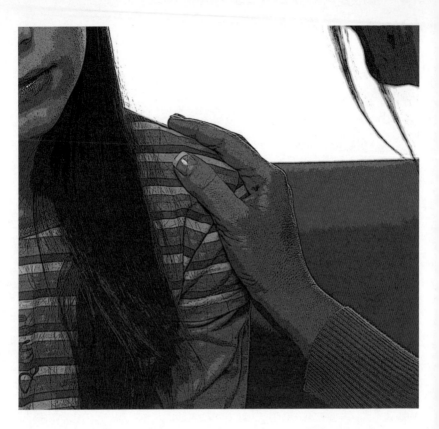

Jessie nodded back. Grateful. It seemed like the first sympathetic thing Jude had said to her for ages.

'It was terrible,' Jessie said. 'But then it was *fine* –' she spread her hands ' – you know – when Dad left.' How could her thoughts be so crystal clear when she was thinking them, so confused when she tried to say them out loud? It made her so mad. 'In fact it was better than fine,' she tried again. 'It was *brilliant*.' She was afraid that she was going to cry again. 'And I thought it would always be like that.' Her voice broke. 'But then, it suddenly wasn't...'

'You mean because of Steve?' Mum said.

Jessie nodded.

'But he's trying so hard to get it right. To make things work, Jess,' Mum said.

'Yes, but don't you see, Mum?' Jessie's voice was high and brittle. 'Don't you see that things are getting bad again? That there's a bad atmosphere. And I hate it.'

Mum put her arm round Jessie and Jessie snuggled up to her. Jude left them to it and went upstairs. 'I'm sorry, luvvy,' Mum said with a deep sigh. 'And yes. Things have been a bit fraught, I admit –'

Jessie was listening hard.

'– I knew it would be hard for you, getting to know someone else,' Mum continued. 'But Steve's not your dad, Jess. And he's not a bit like him. I wouldn't be seeing him if he was.'

There was a lump in Jessie's throat. 'But I'm scared, Mum,' she whispered. 'How do you know he's not like Dad. Aren't you scared?'

There was a long pause now. And Jessie held her breath.

'Starting something is always a bit scary. Even when you're grown-up,' Mum said at last. 'But it doesn't mean we should be afraid of it. You can't go through life like that. And –' she seemed to be struggling with words too '– it's just as hard for Steve, Jess. He's got to get things right this time. He's got his problems too.'

'You mean his kid?' Jessie said.

'It's as hard for her as it is for you,' Mum said. She let go of Jessie.

'Give things a chance, Jess,' she said quietly.

After school the next day Jessie went home with Mel.

In the kitchen, Debbie, Mel's mum, made the girls a drink of juice. She made a cup of tea for herself. Then she sat down with them.

'How's your mum, Jessie?' she asked Jessie.

'I suppose Mel's told you about this guy she's seeing?' Jessie said. Glad to be able to talk to somebody else about it. Wondering what Debbie thought. Wanting her opinion.

'Is it serious?' Debbie said.

'God no!' Jessie said. Wishing she knew.

'It's nice she's got someone to take her out, spoil her a bit,' Debbie said.

Jessie chewed on her bottom lip. 'But you go out with your mates. Mel told me,' she said.

'Yes. But that doesn't mean I wouldn't go out with a guy—' Debbie said, passing round some biscuits. 'That's if there was someone nice out there for me too.' She looked at Mel. 'What do you think, Mel?'

Mel shrugged. 'That's OK by me,' she said.

Jessie had wanted Debbie to say how happy she was with things as they were. Just her and Mel together. And she'd wanted Mel to agree with her mum. The conversation wasn't going as she wanted it to. But then,

she reasoned, Mel had never had someone like Dad to put her off men.

'It always comes back to my dad,' she muttered. Thinking aloud. 'My mum and dad so didn't get on!' she said with feeling. Wondering how much Mel had told Debbie about her father.

'I know, chick. Mel told me what a bad time you had,' Debbie said sympathetically. 'And what you're trying to say now is, because of that, you don't want your mum to see anyone else. Ever?' she added gently.

Jessie didn't know what to say when it was put like that.

'It's understandable,' Debbie continued, leaning over and covering Jessie's hand with hers. 'But it's not fair really. It's a bit hard on your mum, isn't it? Not all guys are bad, thank goodness.'

'Well, why haven't you...?' it slipped out before Jessie could stop herself.

But Debbie didn't seem to take offence. 'It's just never happened for me, yet,' she said. 'But it might. One day. Who knows?' She smiled reassuringly at Mel, then Jessie. 'And if your mum's found a good one now, Jessie, good on her.' She squeezed Jessie's hand. 'I think you should give this man a chance.'

'But – but – he's making all sorts of trouble already. Ever since Mum's been seeing him things have been getting bad again,' Jessie said.

'Give me an example,' Debbie said.

That was easy. 'Well,' Jessie said. 'We had this day out.

In the countryside. It was awful. His kid was a little bra –
monster. Everyone ended up having a bad time.'

'That happens on family days out. Especially with little
kids. It doesn't mean a thing.'

'Then we went to the cinema with him,' Jessie said.
'Just me and Mum. That ended up in trouble too.'

'Why? What happened?'

Jessie looked down at the table. 'They were all over
each other,' she said quietly.

Debbie laughed. 'And it upset you,' she said. 'But isn't
it nice to see your mum happy for a change? Isn't that
better than seeing her miserable?'

'But she wasn't miserable with me and Jude. We
were fine,' Jessie said indignantly. 'Just like you and Mel
are fine.'

'This guy might be lovely,' Debbie said softly. 'I think
you should give things a chance. That's the only way to
find out if it's going to work.'

Chapter Eight

On Sunday morning Jessie heard the Hoover throbbing downstairs. She wondered why. Sunday was usually a lazy day.

By the time she got up, the cleaning was finished and Mum was plumping cushions and arranging things just so.

Jessie wondered what the fuss was about.

Then Mum started preparing lunch.

Anybody would think it was Christmas Day the way she was fussing. A large chicken disappeared into the oven, with all the trimmings. There was a tiramisu sitting on the side defrosting.

'Someone coming to lunch?' Jude said, appearing in the kitchen.

Mum blushed.

So that was it. Jessie should have guessed.

'Yes. Steve and Tracey are coming,' Mum said. She stared at Jessie. 'And I want us to have a nice meal together which we all enjoy,' she said pointedly. 'That's all I'm asking.'

Jessie retreated to her bedroom. Leaned her elbows on the window-sill and stared out of the window.

What was it Debbie had said? '*This guy might be lovely. I think you should give things a chance. That's the only way to find out if it's going to work...*'

She covered her face with her hands. So should she ignore all these worries, then? That niggle that was still insisting that even if he was *lovely*, she still didn't want things to change?

'*It's nice she's got someone to take her out, spoil her a bit,*' Debbie had also said. That had made Jessie feel guilty. Because she couldn't remember her mum ever having much fun.

What were they like together – Steve and Mum? She found herself wondering. How did he treat her? Was he kind to her? Was he fun? Was that why Mum liked him? After all, it was supposed to be teenagers who got things all wrong. Not your mother.

But. How did you know when someone was going to stay nice? she wondered. Or when they were going to turn nasty? That was more to the point.

Jessie shuddered. Then told herself to *stop* thinking like that. She'd just got to be more positive about it. Like Debbie said.

But. Could it, would it, happen again – like with Dad? a small voice still insisted. And was it worth taking the risk? She couldn't help feeling cynical.

Her head was in a turmoil. She had a headache. She

pressed her knuckles into her eye sockets to relieve the pain. Then started wandering round the room. Fiddling with this and that.

She suddenly stopped still, another thought occurring to her. What if he moved in with them? And what if it all went wrong *then*? And they couldn't get rid of him! The thought appalled her.

A car pulled up outside. Jessie jumped up and went to the window. She saw him get out of the car. Then Tracey. He more or less dragged her up the path to the house.

Jessie giggled. She knew exactly how Tracey felt.

But *she* was thirteen, not four, she reminded herself.

Right.

Give things a chance – she told herself.

'Dinner's ready, Jess,' Mum called up the stairs. Jessie came down.

'Hi, Jess,' he said. Which wrong-footed her. Only Mum and her friends called her Jess. 'It's Jessie to you,' she snapped.

It hadn't her taken long to get ratty. She tried a smile at him to make up for it.

Tracey clung to his leg. Head down.

Mum tried to take her by the hand but she held back. Hiding behind Steve.

Jude appeared. 'Hi Steve,' she said. 'Hi Trace.'

'It's Tracey to you,' a voice snapped from behind Steve. Copying Jessie. Well. At least she'd been listening to her,

Jessie thought.

Steve grinned.

Mum held back a laugh.

'Something smells good,' Steve said.

Over dinner there were frequent silences. Reminding Jessie of other painful mealtimes in the past – but she mustn't think about them, she told herself.

Mum's face alternated between looking gooey-eyed at Steve, as if everything was perfect, and looking around, aware that it wasn't.

He looked uneasy.

Tracey, when they persuaded her to sit down at all, kept her head down, as usual, and refused to eat.

Jude kicked Jessie under the table. Jessie didn't look at her. She knew Jude wanted her to try harder. Just like she'd told herself. But it was hard work.

'What school do you go to, Tracey?' Jude asked Tracey.

Silence.

'She goes to Warner Primary,' Steve said.

'Do you like school, Tracey?' Jessie said. Making an effort.

Jude nodded at her approvingly. Mum smiled at her. But Tracey ignored her.

'Jessie asked you if –' Steve said, but Tracey interrupted him.

' – You know I like school, Daddy,' she said. Steve shrugged his shoulders.

'But I don't like this meat,' Tracey said, folding her arms and laying them on the table.

'Leave it then, darling,' Mum said.

So it was *darling* now, Jessie thought. 'You like sausages,' she said.

Mum frowned at her. Careful, she thought.

'Sausages aren't meat,' Tracey said. Red-faced.

'Course they are,' Jessie said. She couldn't help herself biting back. The kid was infuriating.

Tracey got out of her chair and rushed to Steve. 'She says sausages are meat, Daddy,' she cried. Clamouring onto his knee.

'Well they are, pumpkin,' he said, but hurried on, 'not the sort of meat you mean, though.'

'I should have asked you what she liked,' Mum said. 'I didn't think.'

'It's my fault,' Steve said.

Both Mum and he were trying so hard to make everything all right, Jessie saw. And felt guilty. 'Sunday roast's my favourite,' she blurted out. 'Especially chicken.'

'Yuk!' Tracey said.

Jessie could have hit her.

'But you didn't like roast dinners when you were four, Jessie,' Mum reminded her.

'Nearly five!' Tracey said. Accompanied by one of her specially spiteful looks.

'The least you can do is try it,' Jessie said prissily. It was Mum's usual spiel when *she* was being fussy.

'Ahem!' Jude said.

They were all picking on her! Jessie fumed inside.

'Can you cook, Steve?' Jude suddenly asked Steve.

He seemed caught off guard. 'Do you mean me?' he said. 'I'm not a very good cook, actually. But getting better. Needs must and all that. You'll have to come to mine next time and try it.'

His last words hung in the air.

Please! Jessie thought.

But Mum nodded enthusiastically.

Steve smiled back at her. Then he leaned over the table and put his hand on top of hers.

Tracey's bottom lip quivered. 'Yuk!' she said.

Was that the only word she knew?

Steve pulled his hand away. They'd hardly finished lunch when Tracey said she wanted to go home.

Straight away Steve got up and said about getting their coats.

Mum looked disappointed.

Jessie felt sorry for her. Mum had wanted them to play cards after the meal. But she was also relieved. It was hard work trying to be positive. A pity that four-year-olds couldn't try a little harder too, she thought when they left.

'Are all little kids as rude as that?' Jessie asked Mum as she started to clear up.

'She's shy. And confused,' Mum said. 'We've got to make allowances.'

Jessie thought there was plenty of that going on. But it was all going one way.

'Sit down, Mum,' Jude said. 'We'll clear up.'

Chapter Nine

Over sandwiches at school the next day, Jessie brought Mel up to date.

'I really gave it a go, Mel,' Jessie said. 'I remembered what your mum said and really tried. But the kid ruined everything. Every time she opened her mouth there was trouble. She couldn't wait to go home.'

'Poor you,' Mel said.

'And Mum just carried on making excuses for her,' Jessie continued.

'What about him?' Mel asked.

Jessie shrugged.

They finished their lunch. Closed boxes.

'So what happens next?' Mel said.

'Well,' Jessie said and started ticking off on her fingers. 'We've had the day out. And the cinema. And the Sunday lunch.' She stopped counting. 'But yesterday he said something about going round to *his*!' She rolled her eyes dramatically. 'I don't know how much more serious things can get!'

Mel leaned her head on Jessie's shoulder in sympathy.

'It's going to go on and on, isn't it Mel?' Jessie said in a small voice. 'It's not going to go away, is it? Nothing's going to be the same again. And I *loathe it*.'

Mel pulled her up off the bench. 'Come on,' she said. She took her arm and they wandered off.

'You're so lucky,' Jessie said. 'No complications in your life.'

'But you heard what Mum said, Jess. She'd go out with someone too, if she met him,' Mel said.

'You'd know what I mean then,' Jessie said to her with feeling.

That evening, Mum said they'd been invited for lunch to Steve's the coming Sunday.

Hating the thought, nevertheless, a bit of Jessie was curious. Wanting to see where he lived. How. The main part of her didn't want to go though. 'Do we have to go?' she said.

'Jess,' Mum said warningly. 'You're doing it again.'

Jessie sighed.

'Where does he live?' Jude said.

'He's got a flat over by the canal. It's not very big,' Mum said.

'You've been there, then?' Jessie said.

'Yes. Do you mind?' Mum asked.

'Course we don't mind,' Jude said. But Jessie did.

'Like I said, it's not very big,' Mum continued. 'But

there's only him in the week. Him and Tracey at the weekend. He doesn't need a big place.'

'What about his wife?' Jude said.

Jessie held her breath. That was a question she so wanted answering.

'She's living with someone else,' Mum said.

'No wonder Tracey's confused,' Jude said.

Mum looked uneasy.

'What happened? Why did they split up?' Jessie asked. Wanting to know so badly she could hardly breathe.

'His wife met someone else,' Mum said.

'It wasn't his fault then?' Jude said.

'It was her who wanted them to split up,' Mum said. 'It was very hard on Steve. Everyone knowing. She works at the same place as Steve and me. So he sees her every day. That's how Steve and me got talking. He knew about me and your dad splitting up. Something in common. He's divorced now.' The pause that followed was one of those pauses when you had the feeling something important was about to be said. 'I'm seeing a solicitor next week about a divorce, girls,' she finally said.

There was another, shorter, pause. Before Jude said a firm, 'Good.'

Jessie swallowed. 'Good,' she echoed. And hugged Mum. Jude did too.

'Girls together,' Mum said.

Only they weren't anymore, were they? Jessie thought sadly.

The next Sunday morning they arrived at Steve's. The block of flats backed onto the canal. Not bad, Jessie thought.

Steve's flat was very small. Tracey was kneeling on the floor colouring in when they arrived. She ignored them. As usual. There was a tiny kitchen tucked away in a corner of the room.

'The view's nice,' Steve said. Pointing out of the window. Piling their coats on a chair.

Jude and Jessie went and looked out. People were walking along the towpath. A barge meandered past.

'Lovely,' Jude said.

There weren't enough easy chairs for them to sit down, so they sat at the table. 'It's lasagne for lunch,' Steve said. 'Hope you all like it.'

'I don't–' a voice from the floor said.

But Steve interrupted her. 'I know you do, pumpkin.'

Tracey turned her back on them.

Steve got a large dish out of the oven and put it on the table.

'Come and sit up to the table, Tracey,' he said.

'It's usually just me and you, Daddy,' she said. Still colouring furiously.

'It's very nice you having us here today, then,' Mum said.

'It was Daddy wanted you, not me,' she said.

'Come and sit down, pumpkin,' Steve said. In the end he went and picked her up. Sat her down.

'She's in my place,' she said. Looking at Mum.

'It doesn't matter where you sit,' Steve said.

Mum got up. 'I'll swap, I don't mind,' she said.

When they were finally settled, Steve served out steaming portions of lasagne with some salad.

'Mmmm,' Mum said. 'This is gorgeous.'

'I'm not hungry,' Tracey said.

Steve ignored her. 'Had a good week, girls?' he said.

'Boring,' Jude said. She had her GCSEs coming up, so spent most of her time swotting now when she wasn't with Tyrone.

'Jessie got an A grade for an English assignment this week,' Mum said. Smiling at Jessie.

'Well done, Jess,' Steve said enthusiastically. 'I mean Jessie,' he added quickly.

'I read my reading hook to Mrs Angrave and she did a smiley face for me,' Tracey said.

'Well done,' Jude said.

'Good girl,' Mum said.

'I told Daddy, not you,' Tracey said, pouting.

'Trace!' Steve said.

Jude and Jessie looked at each other.

Mum shook her head at Steve. Making allowances again, Jessie thought. The brat seemed to get away with everything.

'Get on with your lunch, pumpkin,' Steve said.

But Tracey was too busy messing her food about. Mixing it up and pushing it round the plate.

'Don't do that,' Steve said.

'Mummy lets me,' she said.

'No, she doesn't. Mummy wouldn't be pleased at all to see you messing your food about like that,' Steve said.

Jessie could see that Steve was getting mad with her at last. Served her right. Her plate looked disgusting.

'I'm not hungry!' she said. Pushing the plate away. 'I wanted to go out today, Daddy,' she said.

'We can't go out every weekend,' Steve said. 'And come on. You must eat something, Trace. It's one of my specials. The only one really,' he added with a grin at Mum.

'Mummy doesn't make me eat anything,' Tracey said. Her voice rising.

'She makes sure you eat something,' Steve said. His voice rising too.

'No, she doesn't,' Tracey insisted. 'Alan doesn't either.'

Steve flinched.

This Alan must be the other man, Jessie thought. And felt sorry for Steve.

He leaned over and took the plate off Tracey. 'No pudding then,' he said.

Tracey put her arms on the table and leaned her head down on them.

The rest of them carried on eating. Jude had seconds. Steve beamed at her. Jessie made an effort.

'Me too,' she said holding out her plate. Mum beamed at her.

'I want some now,' Tracey said. Looking up. Steve got

her plate back and gave it to her. 'I can't eat that,' she wailed.

'There's no more,' Steve said.

'There's none left for me,' Tracey howled.

Steve was red in the face now. 'You should've eaten it when you had the chance,' he snapped.

'Don't shout at me, Daddy. I'll tell Mummy,' Tracey howled.

'I can't eat all of this,' Mum said. 'Do you want some of mine, Tracey?'

'I don't want yours. Yuk!' Tracey said. She leaned over and pushed Mum's plate. It whizzed off the table and landed on the floor with a loud clatter.

For a moment there was complete silence. Jessie bit her lips to stop herself laughing. 'Now that's enough –' Steve yelled at Tracey.

But Mum eyed him urgently. 'It's all right!' she said. Going over to the sink and getting a cloth.

'No, it isn't all right,' Steve said. 'She's not a baby. I'm not letting her get away with that.'

Tracey began to cry noisily. Mum mopped up the mess. Steve collected the other plates up.

'It was lovely,' Jude said enthusiastically.

'Thanks,' Jessie said politely.

Steve put the plates in the sink. Brought the pudding to the table. Lemon meringue pie.

'Your favourite,' Mum said to Jessie.

'And mine,' Tracey said. Stopping crying.

'No pudding for you,' Steve said firmly.

No pudding for you, young lady. You didn't eat your dinner. That's what Mum used to say to her when she refused to eat, Jessie remembered. And then she'd make a terrible fuss. 'She's only little,' she said sympathetically.

But Tracey looked up at her, her eyes full of hate. 'I'm not little,' she yelled.

Brat! 'I was only trying to be nice,' Jessie said sharply.

'There's no need to talk in that tone of voice, Jess,' Mum said.

Even when she tried to be nice, she still came off worse. Jessie was furious.

'I want some pudding,' Tracey cried. Then she opened

her mouth and began to sob loudly.

'I said no,' Steve said.

'Bully,' Jessie said under her breath.

Tracey stopped crying. 'She said bully, Daddy. You're not a bully. She's lying,' she said indignantly.

'I am not a liar,' Jessie said icily.

'For goodness sake, Jess!' Mum said crossly. She was red in the face now. 'You're worse than Tracey.'

Jessie smarted at the criticism. It was so unfair. Tracey leapt down from the table. 'I don't like her,' she sobbed. 'I don't like any of them. And I don't like you, Daddy. I want to go home to my mummy.' Her face was wet. Her nose running. She darted from the room.

'*Pumpkin*,' Steve called after her. Then he went after her.

They could hear him trying to talk her round, but the crying didn't stop. 'I want to go home,' was all they could hear. Over and over.

'We'd better go,' Mum said with a sigh.

They got their coats and left.

Chapter Ten

'I'm going to have a rest,' Mum said when they got home. And disappeared into her bedroom.

'I'm going to meet Tyrone,' Jude said to Jessie. Jessie made a cup of coffee and took it up to Mum.

She knocked on the door and went into the bedroom. Mum lay on the bed, her face to the wall, her back to Jessie, arm crooked round her head.

'Are you all right, Mum?' Jessie said. Putting her coffee down on the bedside table.

Mum sighed. Turned over to face her. 'What a fiasco!' she said.

'That kid's a brat,' Jessie said with feeling.

Mum sat up. 'Don't say that, Jess,' she said. 'She's only a little girl.'

'She's old enough to know if she makes enough fuss she gets her own way,' Jessie said.

'And I know someone else who still tries that,' Mum said.

'That's not fair!' Jessie said. Tears pricking the back of her eyes.

'She's only a little girl. And she's confused,' Mum said.

'Excuses. Excuses. You're always making excuses for her,' Jessie said. 'I'm confused too. What about me?'

'But she's only four. You're thirteen!' Mum said.

Jessie rushed out of the bedroom.

She went to her own room. Leaned on the window-sill. Gazed out. Not seeing.

Her head was spinning.

Mum was ready to make all sorts of excuses for the kid. But none for her. It was obvious where Mum's affections lay now.

Her sister was obsessed by Tyrone. Her mum was obsessed by Steve and Tracey. She wasn't sure how she fitted into things anymore.

She paced round the room for a bit. Lay down on the bed for a bit. Got up and stared out of the window for a bit. Saw a bus at the end of the street.

So!

She grabbed her purse. Then grabbed her quilted jacket out of the wardrobe. Put it on.

Pulled on her woolly hat and tucked her long hair into it. Wound her scarf round her neck. Put her mobile in her pocket. Then ran down the stairs and left the house.

Without telling Mum.

Let Mum worry about *her* for a change.

It was already late afternoon and getting dark.

She wished she could go to Mel's. But Mel and her mum were staying at her gran's for a few days because she was poorly.

She decided to go to the cinema. Except that she'd never been on her own before.

Well. She'd seen a bus, hadn't she? There must be others. Go for it! she told herself.

It felt peculiar. She hardly ever went anywhere on her own, she realised. And she didn't like the feeling. She felt self-conscious.

Well, she told herself, she could turn round and go straight home at any time if she wanted to, couldn't she? Except that that was the last thing she wanted to do and the last place she wanted to be at the moment, wasn't it?

She walked on.

Then stopped to turn her mobile off. She didn't want Mum ringing and finding out where she was, did she? It still felt wicked, though, switching it off. As if she was snubbing Mum. But then, that's exactly what she was doing, wasn't it?

At first she was the only one at the bus-stop. But soon, other people joined the queue.

And if she'd felt self-conscious about being on her own, now it was other people making her feel the same. When an old woman got close to her she didn't like the feeling. Inched away from her. That man – was he looking at her? Those lads. Were they laughing at her? Those two girls with the arms linked, were they talking about her?

She pulled her hat down. Tightened the scarf round her neck. Pushed her hands up the sleeves of her coat and hugged herself. The wind whipped round her legs. It was so cold.

When a bus arrived, she made sure it was the right one, then got on. Relieved.

It took forever. Everyone paying. Despite her not being in a hurry, she felt irritated. And when the bus stopped at every single stop and there was another wait, that irritated her too.

They eventually arrived at the cinema, though. And she marched in as if it was something she regularly did. She scanned the hoards. Choosing an appropriate film. It was that or be refused admission. She'd never looked old enough to fool anyone about her age.

There was over an hour to wait for the beginning of the next performance. But that was good. She wanted to be out long enough to cause loads of worry, didn't she?

She switched her mobile on and texted Mel. Mel texted her straight back. Agog. Telling her to be careful and keep her up-to-date. Jessie felt better knowing that someone knew where she was. Then she switched her mobile off.

She wandered round reading the blurbs to all the films. Not really taking anything in. Time dragged on and on. But at last it was time for the film to start.

She went into the cinema. Surrounded by so many people, she actually felt alone. No one else seemed to notice or care that she was on her own. The back of her throat ached from wanting to cry.

Eventually, though, the film got to her and for a while she forgot her misery. Wallowing in the problems of the kids on screen was good.

As she stole occasional glances around her, she cringed. Remembering how she'd behaved last time she was here. Her behaviour today couldn't be more different. Today, she wanted to be as inconspicuous as possible. To melt into the crowd.

It was nine o'clock when she came out of the cinema. It was bitterly cold outside, and beyond the glare of the cinema lights everything looked very dark.

If she'd been sensitive to people around her before, she was hyper-sensitive now. That gang of lads were laughing at her for sure. Those girls were definitely talking about her. And yes, that old man was certainly staring at her.

She wanted to text Mel again. But she didn't. She kept her mobile firmly in her pocket. Afraid someone might try to grab it.

She walked aimlessly around. Unsure what to do next.

Then she heard her name called. She stopped and looked round. Thinking, gratefully, that it was someone she knew. But then she saw Steve running towards her!

Her instinct was to run away from him, but she was so shocked that she couldn't move.

He rushed up to her. Grabbed her by the arm. 'You stupid kid!' he said.

It felt like he'd hit her. She pulled away from him. Still too shocked to say anything.

'You're coming with me,' he said.

She began to struggle. 'No I'm not,' she said, finding her voice.

'Your mother is worried sick about you,' he said.

He still had hold of her. 'So why didn't she come to find me then?' Jessie said.

'Because I said I would,' he said. His voice tight with anger. 'She rang me in such a panic I couldn't think what had happened. She was certainly in no state to go driving around looking for anyone.'

They'd been talking to each other in quiet, curt voices, almost whispers. Both of them instinctively trying to avoid attention. But suddenly Jessie felt like shouting. 'I'm not going anywhere with you –' she yelled.

Steve began to bundle her along with him. But by now he was getting funny looks from passersby. He dropped her arm.

Jessie darted away from him and ran.

She ran as fast as she could then dived into the middle of a group of people milling around. She let them carry her along till she found herself outside McDonalds.

She rushed in. Panting. Glanced back out. He wasn't anywhere to be seen.

She was glad she'd lost him.

But miserable.

Gritting her teeth so she wouldn't cry, she got in the

queue and ordered the first thing that came into her head. When the food was ready she found a seat and sat down.

But the food choked her.

What was she doing? Mum would be beside herself when Steve told her how she'd behaved. And that she was still out on her own.

Suddenly, panic overwhelmed her and she wanted to go home.

She left the food. Dashed out of the restaurant. Ran for

the bus stop as fast as she could. She wouldn't go home with him. But she would go on her own.

Hordes of people were milling round at the bus stop. Including a gang of noisy youths. There was lots of jostling going on. Jessie flinched. Pictures of muggings flashing through her mind.

'Are you all right?' a woman's voice said. Suspicious eyes peered through the gloom at her. An elderly couple had joined the queue. 'Should you be on your own at this time of night?' the woman said.

Jessie glanced at her watch. It was nearly ten o'clock. She gulped.

A bus pulled up. 'Are you going the same way as us?' the woman said more kindly.

Jessie nodded.

'You'd better get on with us, then,' she said.

The man ushered Jessie and the woman on to the bus. They sat down together on a side seat.

'Don't your parents know where you are?' the woman quizzed her.

Jessie shook her head.

'Had a row, eh?' the man said.

Jessie nodded tearfully.

'Gone off in a huff? Wish you hadn't?' he said.

'Not the first one that's happened to,' the woman said kindly. 'But your parents will be worried sick. You'd best get home as quickly as possible.'

'You'd better be off then,' the woman said as they got to Jessie's stop. 'Go straight home now,' she said as Jessie got off the bus.

Jessie ran all the way.

As she got near to the house she had very mixed feelings. Glad to be home. But afraid.

Mum didn't get angry very often. That had been Dad's speciality. But when she did get angry she was a stinker. And Jessie was sure this would be one of those occasions.

Then she saw Steve's car outside the house.

But she didn't want to see him! For a minute she felt like running past and getting on another bus. But she hadn't got the energy. And she didn't want to be out on her own anymore.

Nervously, she walked up to the back door. Steeled herself and went in.

Through the kitchen. Into the hall.

Then she heard the shouting.

Chapter Eleven

'She ran off!' It was Steve's voice. Urgent. Angry.

'How could you let her?' Mum yelled. Jessie hadn't heard that edge in her voice since Dad's time.

'I hardly *let* her,' Steve yelled. 'Your daughter is a law unto herself.'

'My daughter is a confused little girl,' Mum yelled. Then her voice broke.

'Your daughter is a spoilt brat.' Steve's voice was harsh.

Jessie gasped. So now she knew what he really thought about her.

'–She's had it in for me from the beginning,' Steve continued. 'She was absolutely determined that you and me wouldn't work out. Well. Good on her. Now she's got what she wanted, hasn't she?'

'What do you mean?' Mum said. A note of desperation in her voice.

'Well there's no point in pretending it's ever going to work now, is it Lindsey?' Steve said. His voice suddenly calm. Like he was resigned.

There was a hush.

'It wasn't just Jessie who was the problem,' Mum said. Her voice sort of dull now. As if she was resigned too. 'Your daughter hardly helped.'

'But she's just a baby,' Steve said. 'Your daughter is old enough to know better.'

Jessie pushed the door open. Went in. 'It's all coming out now,' she said. Directing her words to Steve.

Mum rushed up to her. Grabbed her. Hugged her. 'She's thirteen, Steve. Hardly a lifetime of experience to draw on,' she said. Kissing Jessie's head. 'And what experience she's had has been very hard.'

A sob erupted from Jessie's throat.

Mum held her tight.

'Well. Things will be easier for her now, then, won't they?' Steve said. 'Without me, that is. It's over, Lindsey. I can't go on like this.'

He rushed past them both. Out of the room.

They heard the door bang behind him. The car start up.

'I'm so sorry, Mum,' Jessie said. Clinging to her mother.

Mum hugged her back.

It felt so good. But then Mum suddenly let her go and stared at her. 'How could you?' she said. 'How could you worry me like that, Jessie?' Then she started to cry.

Jessie couldn't bear that. 'I'm so sorry, Mum,' she sobbed.

'Anything could have happened to you!' Mum cried.

Jessie felt so guilty.

Neither of them heard Jude come in. 'What on earth is going on?' Jude said and rushed up to Mum.

Mum wiped her eyes. 'It's all right now, Jude. It's all right.'

'What's all right? It doesn't look all right to me,' Jude said. She sounded upset now.

In a haltering voice, Mum told Jude about Jessie running off. Steve following.

Jude glared at Jessie. 'God. Jess, that was a stupid thing to do,' she said.

Jessie was now sitting crying quietly.

'Don't go on at her, Jude,' Mum said. 'I think she's had enough for one day.'

'You look as if you have too, Mum,' Jude said. She put her arm round Mum protectively.

Mum told her the rest.

'So Steve's walked out?' Jude finally said.

Mum nodded. 'It's for the best,' she said quietly.

Jessie's shoulders heaved.

Mum took her up to bed. Saw her into bed.

Jessie was too exhausted to even think. It felt so good to be curled up in her own bed that she soon fell asleep.

The next morning it was almost as if she'd dreamed the whole episode.

But that morning Mum left for work with no make-up on. Her hair a mess. Bags under her eyes.

Jude could hardly wait for her to get through the door

before she started on Jessie. 'Well, are you happy now?' she said.

Jessie didn't know what to say.

Yes, she had wanted Steve out of their lives. She had wanted things to be like they were before Mum started to see him. But she hadn't wanted Mum to be miserable.

All that day, all she could think of was Mum's unhappy face that morning.

When Mum got home from work, she looked even worse. She slumped down in a chair.

Jude fussed round her making cups of tea. Like she was ill.

Jessie didn't know what to do or say. She went up to her room. She was crying so much that she didn't hear Mum come in. But she felt her sit down on the bed.

'Don't cry, luvvy,' Mum said. 'Nothing to cry about now.'

Jessie jumped up. Threw herself at Mum. 'I didn't like Steve because I was afraid it would all start again,' she sobbed. 'I couldn't bear it if anyone hurt you again, Mum.'

Mum held her. 'Steve understood that, luvvy. And he tried to show you that it wouldn't be like that.' Mum smoothed Jessie's tears away with her thumb. 'But it wasn't to be,' she said quietly. 'Another time, another place,' she added sadly.

Chapter Twelve

The next day Mel came home with her after school. Jessie was surprised to find Mum home already. She said she'd left work early. She didn't feel well.

Jude wasn't home.

Jessie looked at Mel. A worried expression on her face. Mel looked at Jessie. They left Mum slumped in a chair and went up to Jessie's bedroom.

At last, sitting face to face on the bed, legs crossed, Jessie told Mel everything. Starting with the lunch at Steve's. Tracey's behaviour, but Mum criticising *her*. 'It was like she didn't care about my feelings,' Jessie said, getting agitated again. 'In the end we had to leave. And when I got home and thought about it I got so mad. That's when I took off.'

Mel grabbed her hand.

'It was so scary, Mel,' Jessie said. 'I can't begin to imagine what it's like being a real runaway!'

Mel squeezed her hand and both girls were silent for a while.

Then Jessie told Mel about getting back home, the row, and Steve leaving.

'Wow!' Mel said. 'That was some day!' She leaned forward and put her arms round her friend. 'But you've got what you wanted, haven't you? It is what you wanted, isn't it? Your mum and Steve splitting up?' she said.

'I suppose,' Jessie said. 'I'm just worried about Mum now, though Mel. You saw how she is.'

They sat quietly for a while.

'I wanted us to be like you and your mum, Mel,' Jessie said. Breaking the silence. 'Just me and Jude and Mum. Except none of it's like that now. Because Jude's got Tyrone. So it's suddenly like I've not got a sister anymore. And Mum. Well. She had Steve. And now she hasn't. And now she's in a worse state than ever.'

The girls hugged.

Chapter Thirteen

Jessie watched Mum becoming more and more lethargic. Like everything was too much trouble. As if she couldn't be bothered with anything. Like she didn't care about anything anymore.

She eventually began to wonder if Mum was ill.

And whatever it was, it must be something serious, she decided. What if she died?

One afternoon after school she sat brooding about it. Jude was revising in her room. And Jessie knew not to disturb her. But by now she was so churned up that she risked it and rushed into Jude's room without even knocking.

Jude was sat at her desk. 'Well, hello Jessie!' she said sarcastically. But she stopped what she was doing.

'I'm worried about Mum,' Jessie blurted out. Hopping from one foot to the other in the doorway.

Jude switched off her music. She always revised to music. Then a slight nod told Jessie to come in. She went and sat on the bed, her legs dangling over the side.

Jude turned her chair round to face Jessie. 'It's depression. Mum's depressed,' she said. 'We did it in class. Hayley Mills said her mum had it. And Miss Burrows asked Hayley if she could describe the illness to us.'

Jessie gulped. So Mum *was* ill.

'Hayley said her mum told her it was like something inside her head shutting down. Switching off. Leaving her sort of brain dead.'

Jessie began to breathe with short shallow breaths. 'It sounds awful!' she gasped. 'How long does it last?'

'It varies, apparently,' Jude said. 'Hayley had to go and stay with her gran in the end while her mum had some treatment. Hayley's gran told Hayley it was because of a *build-up*.'

'What's that mean?' Jessie said.

'Well, apparently Hayley's father left her mother.'

'Like Dad,' Jessie said.

'And now Steve,' Jude reminded her. She leaned forward, staring at Jessie. '*That's* what's really hit Mum.'

Jessie felt guilty. 'A build-up,' she said. Looking down at the carpet.

'I think Mum really liked Steve,' Jude said.

'But then it went all wrong. Just like I was afraid it would,' Jessie said.

'You are the end!' Jude said. Sitting up. 'It was mainly because of you they split up.'

Jessie began to cry. 'It was because of *Dad*,' she said in a strangled voice. 'I didn't like Steve because of Dad.'

Jude sighed. 'When are you going to get it into your head that Steve wasn't Dad and he wasn't like him?' she said.

'And when are you going to get it into your head that he *could've* been like him?' Jessie shouted. She put her hands on her hips.

'You could see he wasn't,' Jude said.

'But how do you *know*?' Jessie insisted. The anger suddenly leaving her, replaced by a desperate need to know the answer.

'Well, we'll never know now,' Jude said simply. 'Will we?'

She came and sat on the bed with Jessie. 'It wasn't all your fault,' she said. 'There was always the brat.'

It was something to hold on to.

'Why don't you put any make-up on these days?' Jessie said to Mum the next morning as Mum got ready for work.

'I can't be bothered. It's too much trouble,' Mum said.

'But it wasn't. Before. You know.'

Mum sighed. She sighed a lot lately.

'You don't go out anymore either,' Jessie continued. 'Couldn't you go out with your workmates sometimes? Like Mel's mum?'

'Look, Jessie. I don't go out. I don't get dressed up. Because I can't be bothered,' Mum said. Her voice flat. Her eyes dull. Her expression like it used to be when Dad was making them miserable.

But since then Jessie had seen another side of Mum. Someone who sparkled. And she missed that side of her.

Then there was the house. No more plumping up of cushions. No more careful arranging.

And food. Jessie tried to remember the last time Mum had made a proper meal. And thought it was probably that Sunday when Steve came to lunch. Which was a long while ago. Nowadays it was takeaways. Or pizzas. Or something on toast. Something easy. Mum didn't have the energy for cooking. She didn't even seem to notice what she was eating. She left most of it. And she was getting thin.

When Mum looked in on her later that night, Jessie sat up in bed. 'Why did you like Steve so much?' she asked.

Mum jumped at the mention of his name. Then she sat down on the bed. 'He was a gentleman,' she said. Her voice soft. Her eyes dreamy.

'But how do you know he was?' Jessie said. 'How do you know he wasn't like Dad?'

Mum leaned over and pulled Jessie close. Jessie snuggled up to her. That was more like the old Mum, she thought happily. Till Mum sighed deeply. 'I'm so sorry about Dad, Jess,' she said.

'You've said that before, Mum,' Jessie whispered. 'It wasn't *your* fault. It was Dad's.' She paused. 'But how do you know Steve wouldn't have turned out the same in the end?' she said.

There was a long silence. Didn't Mum know the answer either, then? Jessie waited.

'Steve respected me. That's why,' Mum said in the end. 'And he made me happy.'

'But why don't Jude and I make you happy anymore, Mum?' Jessie said quietly.

Mum took her time answering again. Then she said, 'Jude's got Tyrone, Jess. And after Tyrone there'll be someone else. And believe it or not, in a few years there'll be someone for you.' She smoothed Jessie's hair. 'Then you'll be out and about too. And that will leave me. On my own.'

The prospect of this happening to Jessie seemed so unreal that she couldn't take it seriously. 'I'm never going to go out with boys,' she said, laying back in bed.

Mum straightened her duvet, the hint of a smile lifting the corners of her mouth. 'When you and Jude are all grown-up,' she said, 'I'll be a long time on my own.'

'But you'll be old then,' Jessie said without thinking.

Mum stopped fiddling with the duvet. And Jessie saw a momentary flash in her eyes. 'I won't be too old to want someone to keep me company,' she said. 'I'm a person in my own right, Jessie. Not just your mum!'

'Sorry,' Jessie said. Flinging herself at Mum again.

'It's all right love,' Mum said. 'It's going to be all right.' She kissed her goodnight.

But was it going to be all right? Was it ever going to be all right again?

When Mum had gone, Jessie chewed over what they'd said.

Why was life so complicated?

Auntie Brenda came round the next day. And when Mum went to make a cup of tea, she took the girls aside. 'I'm very concerned about your mum,' she said, looking worried. 'She gets thinner each time I see her.'

The worry in her voice reflected the worry Jessie was feeling.

'First your dad. Then that Steve coming to nothing. It's no wonder she's depressed,' Auntie Brenda said.

So Jude was right, Jessie thought.

'You two ought to encourage her to get out,' Auntie Brenda said. 'Get her to take an interest in things again.'

'I'm always trying to get her to go out,' Jude said. 'Get a life.'

'She's not been out since she finished with Steve. The day I –' Jessie didn't finish what she was saying.

Auntie Brenda came up to her and lifted her chin. Looking into her eyes. 'That was a mess to be sure, sweetie,' she said. 'But it wasn't all your fault. I blame it on that dad of yours. He ruined things for everybody.'

Good old Auntie Brenda. Even Jude was nodding in agreement. Jessie couldn't hold the tears back any longer.

'There now,' Auntie Brenda said. Patting Jessie's head as if she was still a little girl. 'We don't want you going into a decline as well do we? You've got your mother to think about. We've got to cheer her up somehow, haven't we?'

But how? Jessie thought as they ate biscuits and drank tea.

She was still thinking about that when Auntie Brenda left. The only thing Jessie could think of to make Mum better pointed to *getting Mum and Steve together again!* Even as the thought popped into her head she could hardly believe she'd thought it. Not after all that agonising about him.

But now, when she thought about him, she remembered Steve's easy ways. His smile. The cheeky wink. The way he'd cheered Mum up. The concern he showed Tracey. The fact that he'd come to find her when she'd run away. Even though she didn't want to see him. Grudgingly, she began to see why Mum had liked him so much.

But what could she do about it now?

'About Mum,' she said to Mel at school the next day. 'You'll be fed up hearing about her,' she said anxiously.

But Mel was a good listener. 'Go on,' she said.

Jessie felt choked. She couldn't eat her lunch. She couldn't sit still. 'She was so different when she was going out with Steve,' she said. 'Perhaps your mum was right all along, Mel. Perhaps it would've been all right.'

They wandered round.

'What about if Mum started seeing Steve again and this time I really liked him?' Jessie said.

'But it's not likely to happen now, is it?' Mel said.

'Unless I do something about it,' Jessie said.

The thought sent her into a spin.

It was all she thought about for the rest of that day.

Chapter Fourteen

But what could she do?

She found herself going round and round in circles. Till she remembered that Mum and Steve worked at Enright's. Then she had an idea.

The next morning she told Mum that they had a new project to do at school. And she was going to Mel's after school so they could work together on Mel's computer. It might mean her going there several afternoons on the trot.

Mum said that was fine, as long as she knew where she was.

Which gave Jessie some misgivings. As she had no intention of going to Mel's. Instead, she intended to catch a bus to the industrial estate.

Her idea was to catch Steve after work. Mum had once told her how they worked flexi-time at Enright's. Mum finished work at four-thirty. But what about Steve? It would make life easier if he left at a different time. Please!

So when she left school that day, she caught a bus to the industrial estate.

It was four forty-five by the time she got off the bus. Which meant that Mum would have left work by now. The trouble was, she might have missed Steve too.

Oh well, she thought, as she walked nervously towards Enright's, if she missed him today, she'd come back another day. And another. Till she did catch him.

She waited near the gates. At five o'clock some workers dribbled out of the building. No Steve.

Well, perhaps he finished at five-thirty, then. She waited. Cold. Hungry. Impatient. But determined. At five-thirty there was another dribble of workers. No Steve.

The next half hour seemed to drag on forever. But she waited till well past six o'clock before she gave up. Then, reluctantly, she went to catch the bus home.

So, she thought on the way home, she must get there earlier tomorrow.

At the end of school the next day, she raced to catch a bus to the industrial estate. And this time, arrived at just on four-thirty.

Any minute now Mum could walk out of Enright's. And so might Steve.

Jessie hid behind a tree. Watched. And waited. Sure enough there was Mum. On her own. Head down. Jessie waited till she'd passed.

Then she saw Steve. Walking out with two other men.

Jessie's heart flipped. She was so nervous that it felt like she couldn't move. But she left her hiding place and walked towards them.

As the men drew level with her she said, 'Hello, Steve.'

He looked taken aback. 'Hello Jessie,' he said. Stopped.
'I'll see you tomorrow, Dave, Pete,' he said. They gave
Jessie a curious look and walked on.

There was an awkward silence.

Then. 'What do you want, Jessie?' he said.

Jessie's eyes dropped to the ground. A good question!
'Well,' she mumbled. 'I wanted to say – sorry.'

He didn't say anything.

'Mum's not well,' Jessie said, looking up at Steve. Another pause.

'I had noticed,' he said. 'She looks terrible.'

Jessie saw the concern in his eyes and forced herself to continue. 'Do you still like her?' she asked. Holding his gaze now.

Steve's eyes suddenly blazed. 'If it's any of your business–' he said, '–and I don't know why I should tell you anyway. But yes, of course I do. For what it's worth.'

She'd gone over in her head the way this conversation might go, but she still didn't know what to say next. 'I'm sorry,' was all that came out. Again.

He shrugged. As if it didn't matter. And her getting in such a state! 'OK,' he said finally. 'But it's not really important now is it, Jessie?'

He walked off towards the car park.

Jessie walked dejectedly back to the bus-stop.

What had she achieved? she asked herself. She'd told him she was sorry. That was good. And she knew now that he still liked Mum. That was the main thing she supposed. So she felt a bit more cheerful about it. But she'd have to come back and try something else, wouldn't she?

Just after four-thirty the next day she was hidden again, watching Mum go by. Then waited for Steve.

This time he came out on his own. When he saw her again he shook his head. 'What?' he said.

'Will you come to tea on Sunday?' she said. She'd rehearsed this all the way there. And it still sounded as stupid as it had in her head. But she didn't care.

He grinned a wry grin. 'What are you up to, Jessie?' he said.

'You said you still like her. And she still likes you,' Jessie said quickly.

'Yes?' Steve said. His eyes narrowing.

'Well.' She stared back at him. 'It would be a good idea if you came to tea, then, wouldn't it?' she said.

'If your Mum wanted me to come to tea,' he said, 'she could ask me herself.'

Jessie's voice was shaking now. 'But you're not even talking to each other, are you?' she said. 'So – that's why I came. To ask you *for* Mum.'

'So she doesn't – exactly – know about this invitation?' he said.

Jessie blushed. Shook her head.

He lowered his chin and looked up at her. 'And are you going to – tell her?'

She cleared her throat. 'Don't know,' she said. It sounded like a squeak.

He made a noise like a hiccough. Surely he wasn't laughing at her? 'And this is all your idea then?' he said. There was heavy emphasis on the *your*.

'Yes.'

'*You* want me to come?' he said. Emphasis on the *you*.

'Yes,' she said. 'I want you to come.' She was beginning to feel more confident now.

'And Tracey?' he asked. 'Is she invited too?'

Jessie bit her bottom lip. 'It might be better if you came on your own,' she said.

Another funny sound came from his throat. 'Actually. Tracey's not coming this weekend,' he said. 'So.' He got his car keys out of his pocket. 'I'll think about it. Now. Do you want a lift home?'

She shook her head.

'Where does your Mum think you are, Jessie? She'll be worried sick if she doesn't know,' he said anxiously.

'It's all right. She thinks I'm at my friend Mel's,' Jessie said quickly.

'So I can give you a lift, then. Drop you off at the end of the street?' he said. 'Our little secret.'

This time when he winked at her she smiled back at him. 'Thanks,' she said.

Chapter Fifteen

She couldn't wait to tell Jude. See what she thought.

'Surprise,' she said, going into her room as soon as she got home. 'Steve's coming to tea on Sunday. I think. He didn't promise. But he said he'd think about it. That usually means yes.' She stared defiantly at Jude.

'What?' Jude said.

'I asked him to come to tea. And he's thinking about it,' Jessie said. Grinning at the look on her sister's face.

'What?' Jude said as if she still hadn't taken it in.

Jessie giggled. It wasn't often she got to shock her sister. 'I went to Enright's after school,' she said slowly. Jude's eyebrows were nearly touching her hair. 'I hid from Mum. Then I waited for Steve. We got talking. I asked him to come to tea.'

'You got talking!' Jude said. 'I'm gob-smacked!' Then she suddenly chuckled.

'You're pleased, then?' Jessie said. Chuckling too. Jude shook her head as if she still didn't understand.

'You've got over your obsession about him, then?' she said.

Jessie pouted. 'Well, I had to do something,' she said. 'Mum being depressed and all that.'

'God! It's a good job Mum didn't know where you were,' Jude said. 'She'd kill you. For going off on your own, I mean.'

'But she didn't know, did she?' Jessie said. 'So what about this tea, then?'

'It's a bit naff isn't it? Asking him to tea!' Jude said.

'I couldn't think of anything else,' Jessie said. 'Do you think I should tell Mum?' she said anxiously.

Jude frowned. 'Best not,' she said. 'He might not even come. We don't want her getting in more of a state than she is already.'

'I agree,' Jessie said. Relieved. 'I've got it all worked out. I'm going to ask Mum to let me *supposedly* ask Mel and her mother to tea. Sort of a thank you for going there and using their computer. Then we have an excuse for getting the food and everything. And we can get Mum to dress up and all that.'

'You little schemer!' Jude said. 'Let's just hope he comes.'

Mum wasn't keen on Mel and her mum coming to tea. But agreed anyway. Like she didn't really care.

'It'll be all right, Mum,' Jessie said. 'I'll get everything ready. And Jude said she'll help.'

On Sunday afternoon, Jessie asked Mum what she was going to change into. Mum said she was all right as she was. But Jessie desperately wanted her to make more of an effort.

'Mel's mum always looks so nice,' she said.

It worked. Mum said she'd go and find something to change into. 'Anybody would think it was someone important coming,' she said.

Jessie caught Jude's eyes and they pulled a face at each other.

'I'll put your hair up, Mum,' Jude said and went upstairs with her.

When Mum came back downstairs Jessie felt like crying. Mum had lost so much weight that her skirt hung on her. Her cheeks were hollow and her eyes looked huge in her pale face. She looked beautiful, though. She'd put some make-up on and Jude had done her hair.

'You look great, Mum,' Jessie said. Aware of the clock ticking away. Listening for the sound of a car.

Had she done the right thing? And would he come? What would Mum do when she saw him? Would she be angry? Would she get upset? The worst thing would be if Mum was upset. Jessie so wanted her to be pleased.

Perhaps she should warn her now? Give her time to get used to the idea. But she couldn't bear the thought of her being disappointed. Best let things just happen.

Then she heard a car. She steeled herself as the door bell sounded.

'I'll go, Mum,' Jessie said, stiff with tension. But Mum beat her to it.

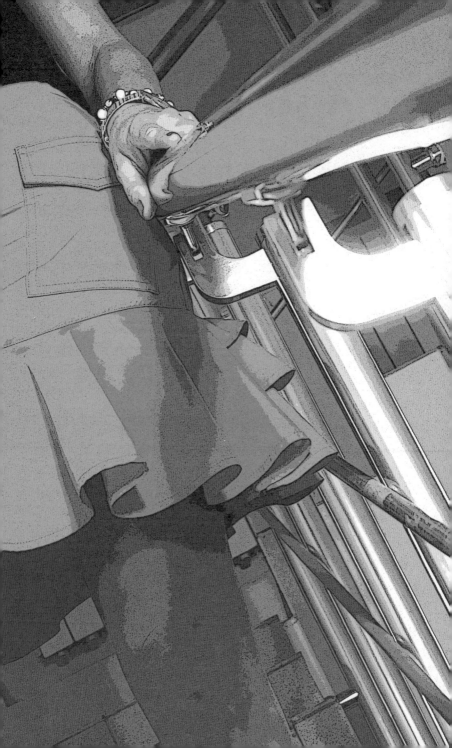

Chapter Sixteen

Mum stared at him as if she'd seen a ghost.

Then a flush spread over her face. It made her look prettier than ever.

He looked as if he wanted to grab hold of her and never let her go.

So far so good. Jessie crossed her fingers behind her back.

'What are you doing here?' Mum said at last.

'I've come for tea,' he said matter-of-factly. Then winked at Jessie.

Mum just stood there.

'You haven't told her, Jessie, have you?' Steve said.

'Let him in then, Mum,' Jessie said quickly.

Mum looked at Jessie. Wide-eyed. 'You knew about this, didn't you?' she said. 'I don't understand!' Her face flushed pinker than ever. 'Are Mel and her mum coming too?' she asked.

Jessie shook her head.

'It was an excuse to get you togged up,' Jude said.

Grinning.

'And worth it!' Steve said appreciatively.

'I asked him because...' Jessie began. Dried up.

Mum gave Jessie a quick, unsure look. 'Yes?'

'Everybody's so worried about you, Mum,' Jessie said quickly. 'I decided it was up to me to–'

Steve made a funny noise.

Jessie's temper flared. Was he laughing at her again? She put her hands on her hips. Stared at him.

'All right.' He held his hands up. 'I'm sorry.'

'What for?' Mum said. Suddenly finding her voice. 'You've not done anything wrong. *You* never did anything wrong,' she added.

He put an arm round her. And she buried her head in his shoulder.

At one time it would've made Jessie heave. Today, she found herself welling up.

'Let's go and make the tea, Jess,' Jude said. And they went into the kitchen giggling.

Jessie was on too much of a high to eat anything. It felt so good to have got things right for a change.

Several times Steve or Mum started talking at the same time. Then they apologised. Laughed. Started again.

Jessie and Jude grinned at each other.

They talked about work. As if they never saw each other there. Then Mum asked Steve about Tracey. 'Where is she today?' she asked.

'She's with her mother this weekend. She's still being

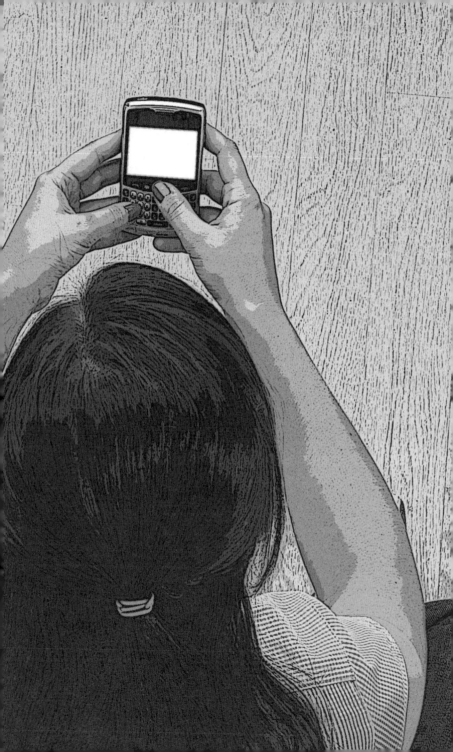

bloody-minded.' Steve glanced at Jessie and away again. Jessie blushed. 'But things are gradually settling down. Not quite so many tantrums,' he said.

Then he asked the girls about school. They told him about their favourite subjects. What they liked and didn't like. What they were good at.

Conversation flowed like it had never done before. And for the first time Jessie relaxed in his company. She kept looking at Mum, and couldn't help feeling smug. Mum was smiling so much it looked like she'd never stop. And the sparkle was already back in her eyes.

When Steve had gone, Jessie went to her room and texted Mel. Then she lay back on her bed and closed her eyes. It felt like she was starting to breathe easy again at last. The dull ache of worry seeping away.

Mum came into her room. 'Thank you, Jess,' she said. They hugged.

Jessie felt a delicious feeling creep through her. She was happy. 'You really like him, don't you, Mum?' she said.

'Yes, Jessie. I'm not going to pretend I don't,' Mum said.

'That's OK,' Jessie said.

'Is it?' Mum said quietly. 'And does that mean you don't mind me seeing him again, then?'

'After all the trouble I've gone to I'd be disappointed if you didn't,' Jessie said. And then she told Mum about going to Enright's and everything.

Mum's eyes nearly popped out of her head.

The following week, Steve popped in several times. And each time, Jessie felt more confident that she'd done the right thing. As Jude had said, things were going to be all right.

Except for one thing.

Chapter Seventeen

There was still the problem of Tracey.

Mum suggested they all went to the zoo at the weekend. 'It's important Tracey gets to know us better,' she said to the girls.

Jude told Mum she had exams next week. She'd got to revise.

That left Jessie and Tracey.

Jessie wondered what Tracey would be like when she saw them again. Remembering her behaviour the last time at Steve's flat, she thought she knew the answer to *that*.

Steve called for them.

Jessie got in the car first. And when she saw the protruding bottom lip and the downcast eyes she knew that nothing had changed.

'Hi Tracey,' she said in a cheerful voice.

Nothing.

But, she told herself, Tracey's behaviour was not going to rile her today. She was determined to get through the day without a row. 'What do you want to see at the zoo?' she said. Trying to get Tracey talking.

'Nothink,' Tracey said into her lap.

'What's your favourite animal then?' Jessie persevered.

'Nothink,' Tracey said.

Jessie felt herself getting mad but refused to give into it. She took a long breath.

'I don't like the zoo,' Tracey said. Pulling her knees up and burying her head in them.

'Tracey wanted to stay home today,' Steve said. Looking sheepish.

'I didn't,' Tracey wailed. 'I wanted to go to the zoo with you. Just me and you, Daddy. I didn't want to go with them.'

Them sounding like the plague. Jessie bit her lip to stop herself retorting.

Steve caught her eyes in the rear mirror and he smiled sympathetically.

When they got to the zoo, Tracey clung to her dad's hand. Refusing to leave him for a minute. Mum said that she and Jessie would go off somewhere on their own.

'Let's give them a bit of time together,' she said.

It was OK by Jessie. It was nice having Mum to herself.

'I'm really proud of the way you're growing up lately,' Mum said.

Jessie felt really good. They linked arms. When they rejoined Steve and Tracey, Steve and Mum went to get some drinks. Jessie had another go at placating Tracey, but she was having none of it. She stared at Jessie. 'He's my daddy, not yours,' she said.

Jessie counted to ten.

At the end of the day, Steve dropped Mum and Jessie off. And as Mum said goodbye to Tracey, she said, 'Perhaps you could come and visit us here, Tracey, next time you stay with Daddy?'

Jessie cringed.

Tracey dropped her bottom lip.

Jessie hadn't been in long when Jude came into her room. 'Well?' she said. 'How did it go?'

'That kid!' Jessie said. 'She was as pig-headed as ever. But I did try.'

'Good for you,' Jude said.

Jessie clasped her hands between her knees. Hunched her shoulders.

'Now you're not getting stressed out again, are you?' Jude said.

'But she's a nightmare, Jude. And you'll never guess. Mum said about her coming here next time she visits Steve,' she said. 'Imagine putting up with her here!'

'She's only a little kid, Jess. She'll come round. It'll be all right,' Jude said. Sounding just like Mum. But Jessie didn't mind that today. It was what she needed to hear.

Apart from Tracey, things were soon going well. Jessie was getting used to having Steve around. She found herself warming to him more and more.

Then one night, when they were watching telly, Steve wanted to watch football. But Jessie wanted to watch *Eastenders*. Jessie was mad when Mum said it was only fair that Steve watched the football. 'You can watch the omnibus edition of *Eastenders* at the weekend,' she said.

'But we always talk about it at school. I want to watch it now,' Jessie snapped. And when she saw she was getting nowhere with Mum, she stormed upstairs in a huff.

It was the first row.

The next thing, Steve came up and was knocking on her bedroom door. She was still mad. But glad he'd followed her. He came in and said he wanted her to come back

downstairs. That it was OK for her to watch *Eastenders*. Which made Jessie feel guilty. So she said, no. It was OK if he watched the football. She'd got homework to do anyway. And then they laughed.

It felt good. And in a funny way made Jessie feel more secure.

Then one day, Jude said about Tracey, 'You might have to get used to her being around here quite a lot soon, if Steve moves in.' While that was sinking in, Jude carried on. 'It looks like Mum and Steve will want to be together, don't you think, Jess? And we couldn't move into his tiny flat. It's too small. So he'll have to come and live with us.'

She made it sound so matter-of-fact.

It had occurred to Jessie, of course, that Steve and Mum would want to live together one day. But she hadn't thought it through. She certainly hadn't thought about Tracey! 'God,' she said, 'fancy having to put up with her here.'

Jude laughed.

When Jessie was on her own she started to brood again. Change worried her. And Steve moving in with them would be a very big change. Without Tracey complicating things.

The more she thought about Tracey, the more she doubted that she'd ever fit in with them.

Then something hit her like a thunderbolt.

Chapter Eighteen

As soon as Mum came home Jessie tackled her.

'Mum. Is Steve coming to live with us?' she asked.

Mum looked taken aback by the question. 'Let me get my coat off,' she said.

Jude had come downstairs to get a drink. 'Jessie!' she said. 'That's up to Mum and Steve.'

'Sorry, Mum,' Jessie said. 'But I've got to know.' Mum took her coat off. Went through to the sitting room. The girls followed her.

'Sit down Jess,' Mum said. Jessie perched on the edge of the sofa. Mum sat down next to her. 'Why the panic?' Mum said. Pausing. 'And would you mind if Steve did move in?' she asked gently.

'No. No – that's all right,' Jessie said.

Mum looked relieved.

'But–'

Mum looked worried. 'But what?' she said.

'There's always a but with you, Jess,' Jude said.

'Yes,' Jessie said. 'And this time it's a big but!' Her eyes were blazing. 'Because Tracey would come to stay as well, wouldn't she?'

Mum nodded. Looking puzzled now. 'Yes,' she said. 'For weekends. In her holidays.'

Jessie gulped. 'And we've only got three bedrooms, haven't we?' she said.

'Ah!' Mum said. 'I see where this is going now.'

'Where will she sleep, Mum?' Jessie asked in a high anxious voice.

'Well.' Mum hesitated. 'There's room for another bed in your room, isn't there, Jess?' she said.

'I thought as much!' Jessie said through clenched teeth. '*My* bedroom! That's what it means, Mum. Mine. I'm not sharing my bedroom with anyone. Especially not that brat!'

'Jessica!' Mum said.

'So where else can she sleep? In the garage?' Jude said. 'Lighten up, Jess.'

But Jessie didn't think it was funny. 'What about your room?' she said furiously. But knowing the answer. She folded her arms and pouted. 'I wish I was the oldest,' she said. 'Anything important and you always get your way. Just because you're the oldest.' She lowered her head.

Mum tried to calm her down. 'It will only be for short periods, luvvy,' she said. 'I don't know what else to suggest.' She put her arms round Jessie. 'If Steve did come to live here, Jess, Tracey would be part of the family too.' She was pleading now. 'A sister,' she

added quietly.

A shudder went through Jessie. It was the final straw! She really hadn't thought it through, had she? 'But I don't want another sister!' she yelled. Pushing Mum's arms off her.

Jude came and sat the other side of Jessie. Put her arms on Jessie's shoulders. Waited till Jessie looked at her. 'A *little* sister, Jess,' she said. Looking at Jessie knowingly. 'Think about it. You'll be her *big* sister.'

Jessie thought. And felt her shoulders begin to relax.

That was true. And that wasn't so bad.

Not being the youngest any more, she could do a bit of bossing of her own, couldn't she?

She straightened up. The beginnings of a smile playing round the corners of her mouth.

Mum and Jude were looking at her anxiously.

'Yesss!' Jessie suddenly said. Shaking her fists. And grinning widely.

Mum and Jude smiled at each other.

'Look out Tracey!' Jude said, looking at Jessie. 'She is *not* going to get things all her own way, is she, little sister?'

'No way!' Jessie said and laughed.

If you enjoyed reading *No Way!*, look out for other titles in the *On The Wire!* series:

CyberFever by Gillian Philip
Mamie's not stupid - she's heard all about the dangers of Internet chatrooms. But she's met Sam12, a boy with an amazing knowledge of films that rivals her own. And she thinks he might be cute, too. So what's the harm in suggesting they meet up?

You Can Do it! by Jill Atkins
He's the school's star football player and all round popular guy. Jack's impatient to make the most of his activity week in Snowdonia - but then tragedy strikes. How does he cope when his world is suddenly upended?

Seeing Red by Jill Atkins
Vicky this, Vicky that! It's always the same - and Vicky can't stand it for a second longer. So she packs her bags and leaves the nagging behind. But while life on the streets provides welcome relief from her parents, it brings new dangers and hard lessons to be learnt.